My Service Person

"A service dog's story"

Written by Jake Taylor
Illustrated by Alex Peterson

My Service Person

Written by J.Taylor

Illustrated by A. Peterson

Hi! My name is Tobin.

When I was just a puppy, a very nice lady named Beth visited me, my brothers, and my sisters.

She told me that I could help some very special people.

I always loved helping my family so I kissed my mom and family goodbye and joined Freedom Dogs.

We traveled to San Diego on a big flying machine.

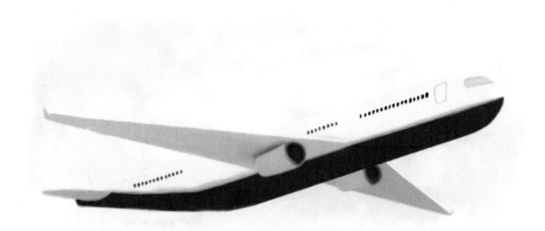

It was very loud and scary, but I wanted to
show Freedom Dogs I was brave. So I sat quietly,
and told myself, "Be brave, just be brave!"

After awhile, we landed and the noises
stopped. Then, we went riding in a car - I like
cars! Lots of smells come in the windows.

I forgot to mention, dogs have very powerful
noses. I can smell about as well as you can
see.

Today was my first day of training and boy was it fun! Can you believe they gave me treats for just sitting and being smart!

I love treats, don't you? Every time I got something right, I got a treat!

This was a very busy morning training; time for a puppy nap.

I trained every day, like going to school. My trainer, Atsuko, is like a second mom to me. She is very smart and teaches me words and what they mean like "place, heal, stay, and bananas!"

I LOVE BANANAS! They are my favorite!

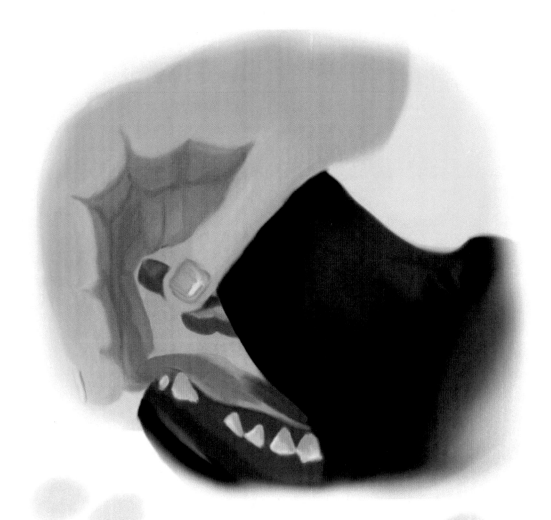

After six months I was getting the hang of all the training, and I had been to classes where special people called 'heroes' would visit us. We would help teach them to become dog trainers too and they usually gave us lots of treats!

Today was different though, they put me with a hero named Jake. He was very big, but kind and gentle. He gave me treats also, but liked to challenge me a bit. I like challenges.

He had me climb onto rocks and stand very still. He said that I looked like super dog! I liked that!

Then he gave me one of my favorite things, a big
stick! I love sticks, you can throw them, chew
on them, and play tag with them!

I began working with Jake every week, I'd teach him something, and then he'd show me something. We were a good team!

He could even make my tennis ball disappear, it was a cool magic trick.

We started to go places together, the store, the doctor's office, the mall, and even restaurants.

Everywhere we went, he seemed to not like the attention that we got.

People aren't used to seeing dogs like me. It was very hard for him.

I like to distract the people so they don't see him.

I discovered golf today! Jake is really good at golf; he can hit the ball really far! It is quiet on the golf course and I like all the smells and trees.

I even got to ride in a golf cart.

But, I had to be quiet and listen...

Sometimes I help him find the golf ball by using my nose!

The more time that Jake and I spent together, the more I could see that he had seen some scary things. He wouldn't talk about it, but I could tell he was very brave.

When we would go on walks in the woods it was
amazing, and he would be so happy. He seemed
to forget about the bad things he had seen. I
knew, right then, that was my purpose at
Freedom Dogs, keeping the heroes like Jake
from thinking about scary things.

I learned that when people would talk to him, it was about those scary things. So I learned to watch him and remind him to be happy.

I'd nudge him at first, then I try to tell him let's go for a walk.

If that didn't work, I would make him go for a walk. He understands me.

He's alone a lot, but not when we're together! I wish people could understand heroes like I do. They have been brave for us all.

About the Author and Illustrator

Jake and Tobin

Jake served three tours in Iraq and Afghanistan from 2004-2008. After suffering a severe traumatic brain injury in 2015, Jake began to suffer from short term memory loss and severe PTSD. His executive functions and social reasoning suffered, causing severe depression.

Jake has been a member of the Freedom Dogs family for almost 4 years. Tobin, his faithful shadow, never leaves his side.
Through the positive behavioral training that the service members are taught in handling the dogs, Jake developed his own methods of cognitive behavioral therapy.

His hope is to create a program that treats PTSD patients faster and more effectively than current treatments, without the use of pills and medications.

Alex and Koda

As a U.S. Marine, Alex served two tours in Iraq and two tours in Afghanistan. As a result, he lived with undiagnosed PTSD for over a decade.

Alex and Specialty Trained Service Dog Koda united as partners for life in 2018. After 13 years of service, Alex was retired from the U.S. Marine Corps shortly after being diagnosed with severe PTSD.
Koda was instrumental in Alex's recovery and his transition from the Marine Corps into civilian life and later on into college. Today, the two lead a healthy, happy life style with most days spent outside in the sun learning and training.

Alex continues to work with Freedom Dogs and is pursuing a career as an artist. Alex's focus is to bring awareness to the troubles we all face as result of trauma and broadcast that there is help available.

Freedom Dogs is headquartered in Oceanside, California just outside Camp Pendleton Marine Base.

Founded in 2006, its mission is to speed the recovery and enhance the lives of wounded military heroes through the use of Specialty Trained Service Dogs.

HEROES FOR FREEDOM DOGS OUR HEROES

For more information visit the Freedom Dogs website:

www.freedomdogs.org

Follow them on Instagram: freedomdogsorganization

Post Traumatic Purpose LLC.

Made in the USA
Las Vegas, NV
31 October 2022

58501523R00017